SOUL
SEARCHING

Literary Art From and
For a Searching Soul

SHANNON JENKINS

Soul Searching: Literary Art From and For a Searching Soul
Copyright © 2023 by Shannon Jenkins

ISBN: 978-1-958707-04-3

First Printing March 2023

Printed in the United States of America

For Inquiries:
sunjae.dvhour@gmail.com
IG: sunnybryte40
FB: Shannon Jenkins

DEDICATION

Dedicated to the young lady who did not give up when the weight of the burdens lay heavy upon her backside. She leaned forward but did not fall; she put one foot in front of the other and balanced herself. To the young lady who didn't let the blurred vision from the tears blind her from the vision of her goal. She shifted her energy, regained a clear conscious mind then strapped down those burdens upon her back and throughout her journey, she began to drop them, one at a time. To that young lady who wasted no time letting the past stay just that, so that her future could be built, you have come a long way from where you were now feeling infinite self-love without an ounce of guilt. You did it!! I am so proud of you and without a doubt, this is just the beginning.

A special thanks to my sister Trivia Jenkins and my mother, Valerie Jenkins. You both have watched my story play out from the beginning through all of my challenges, stumbles, and comebacks. You both were there to give that second voice I needed to keep moving and I want you both to know that I love you.

To my friends and the others that I have had the pleasure of crossing paths with whom have also played a part in this journey. Your encouraging words helped spark my motivation and through encouraging conversations I kept moving forward. While pursuing and not giving up, when I was at an all-time low climbing my way up a rabbit hole you lent a helping hand. Small things do make a big difference, thank you!

Patricia Knight
Kathleen Kohut
Alan and Kate Henderson (Medix School)
Janae Wilkerson
Eddie T.
Kyoho Hanamori, Cheryl Hicks, and all the Tranquili-Chi Center Team
Renee Murray
Tracy Drake
Randy Cornish
Vickie Collette

TABLE OF CONTENTS

UNITY

Together we stand;
united we fall.
I will never leave you; I'll give you my all.
My heart and soul belong to you
just as yours belong to me.
We will always be together as one in
unity.
Understand that times will get hard, and sometimes they may get
worse...
But in my eyes, this time, you will always come first.
Pain and sorrow will come, that's all a part of life;
I love you more than you can imagine,
I just want things to be right.
We will be together one day,
and you will soon see;
we will stand strong together,
as one, in
Unity.

January 12, 1996

ALL I NEED

---

*All I need, all I want is someone for me. I'm not to be shared and
not to be deceived.
All I want is that special someone who can somehow make me
believe that there is more to life than the birds and the bees.
All I need is someone that knows when to say
that there's still a little princess that comes out of me
each and every day.
All I want is someone who knows how to make me smile, someone
who can make me feel as if I'm floating in the clouds. That
someone who will know how to comfort me whenever I cry,
this someone will hold the special ingredient that makes him
always turn out just right.
This special someone will hold me in his arms at the end of every
night.
All I need is someone who wants to be my friend, someone that I
can be with and trust up until the end.
If I ever find this special someone, I promise never to let him go.
I'll promise to take care of him and always let him know; that ever
since he came around, my life hasn't skipped a beat, that during
our time together, I have figured out that he is
all I'll ever need.*

December 23, 2001

SKY

The sky is the limit for everything we do.
Sweetheart, the sky is the limit for me and for you!
I'll stand by your side, and I promise to hold your hand,
but the question in my head is:
are you a good man?
I'm a very good woman and I'll always demand respect;
I deserve only the best, never will I settle for less.
I want you to know before I say goodbye, that all of your answers
rest in the sky. Believe in me for I will believe in you and
never forget
the sky is the limit for everything we do!

September 30, 1995

HOMELESS

No expressions, just blank faces.
Shivering and sick, too ashamed to beg and still too proud to cry.
Ten black alleys, decisions...decisions... No blankets, sheets, or food.
He sleeps with delicious thoughts of chestnuts by the fire, and the
oven-roasted turkey fed only by smelly garbage.
A world so far from ours, and yet it's close enough to touch.

A world crowded with starving souls,
empty and draped in odor.
His tattered found coats are proudly well-worn.
The chortle of others drowns the day into night, shattered hopes
and dreams, conqueror of pain.
Soldiers of a wrecked people and each has a name...but no one ever
asks.

These are our people,
no matter their color or creed.
Wake up, wake up, wake up!
Was it all just a dream?

He was eating turkey by the fireplace and drinking wine with
family and friends.
He was warm and clean, watching the snow fall through the
window beam.
But was it just a dream?

He's laughing and bonding; it's been so long since he has seen them.
But was it all just a dream?
He's still hungry... He's still cold...
He still has that pain in his chest that just won't go away... But was it all just a dream?
?
?
?
Yes,
He's still homeless...

November 17, 2000

ECSTASY

What a wonderful night it would be
if only you would spend the night.
Stay with me my sweet, caress me
hold me tight.

We can share our secret thoughts
and perform our wildest desires.
Take off your clothes.
Feel the Fire...

It doesn't matter about our dirty minds; ecstasy has no limit or
time.
I want to feel you deep into me
Come on, don't stop...
Oooh, you're hurting me...

I feel it baby, how much you really care,
Oooh... your tongue
...feels so good down there.

Don't get up,
I like it this way.
tell me now that
you're going to stay.

I want you here right by my side,
and these wonderful feelings
I just can't hide.
Don't leave me tonight,
I've already prepared your side.

March 15, 1994

See You Later

At a time like this,

everything must be true,
you will always be in my heart,
and I will always love you.

Leaving you is like leaving my heart behind, someday in the
future,
you will once again be mine.

A day without you
is a day of despair
with no beautiful dreams,
just a cursed nightmare.
How often I yearn for gentle hands
thine no longer caressing me,
no longer mine.

Although this relationship is coming to a pause, believe me, it's all
happening for a very good cause.

This is not the end,
just a new beginning;
brighter dreams and bigger hopes
will bring us together

before you know it.

This relationship will never end;
as long as the heart still beats
we will always be friends.
Listen to your heart
it never lies,
and if our destiny passes stormy weather
the greatness of life
will let us again be together.

July 26, 1994

DID I SAY THANK YOU?

---

*His grace, his mercy, gave me the strength to carry on. His love, his
patience, gave me an understanding heart.
Did I say, "Thank you, lord?"
for all that you've done.
Did I say, "Thank you, lord   ?"
for giving your son?
You saved my soul, and every day, I pray
that you keep me whole and bring me home someday.
Did I say, "Thank you, lord?"
Did I say, "Thank you?"
Some people forget
you're the one that makes this life of ours possible.
Others forget your love
and that you're the all-powerful.
You've shown me the way that I must take,
giving unconditionally your love to get me through.
You said that I'm your child,
a child of God that the devil just can't move.
Some don't understand the power behind your name,
taking life for granted and living in vain.
My life is not mine, but yours, you see,
because lord, you did it all just to save me.
Did I say, "Thank you, lord?"
for all that you've done.
Did I say, "Thank you, lord?"*

for giving your only son?
You saved my soul, and every day, I pray,
that you keep me whole
and bring me home someday.
Did I say, "Thank you?"
I'm eternally grateful, and I will forever praise your name.
Living right by you, lord,
and telling others to do the same.
By the way, Lord, did I remember to say, "Thank You?"

June 12, 1998

My Friend

In my time of need, you were always there. When I felt it was all
over you would say
"He's not going to put more on you than you can bare."

I thought of many things that would bring all this pain to an end.
Today I am still smiling, standing strong because of you,
My Friend.

When my tears would slowly run down the side of my face,
your shoulders wiped my tears away.

As always, you were there for me to lean on, wrapping your arms
around me to say... "What doesn't kill you shall strengthen you
again someday."
Today, my head I hold very high
and I thank you for the helping hand that you would lend.
Through all of my trials and tribulations,
I must say you've been the greatest friend.
Now that I've come this far and with my boxing gloves on,
the life you said was ahead of me, I can surely say that you weren't
wrong.

Life can sometimes be a never-ending journey,
a constant battle of things you can't fix,

but with my faith, family, and friends I will never give up or quit.

*I thank you again for all that you've done for me
and the encouraging words you would give.
With each word bringing me one step back to a sound mind,
again I say, "thank you"
My Friend.*

I am the luckiest person to have someone like you in my life,

one who has helped me to see that a future can be reached and can be bright.

You said you would be around until the end,

I trust and believe you simply because you have been an Awesome Friend!

October 29, 2004

Is This What You Want Me to Do?

I opened up just like he said,
"Lift them higher,"
and he lifted my legs.
I needed to feel his hips against mine,
but he was procrastinating,
wasting my time.
Teasing my body without an inch untouched,
he dampened every crease of me
with the tighten of my clutch.
Looking up at me with his sleepy little eyes,
he was enjoying my shouts, my tears, my outcries.
My body was weak, and I wanted to rest,
but he whispered in my ear, "No, baby, not just yet."
He lifted me up and turned me around,
scratched down my back, and with sweat dripping, he made these
little sounds.
Caressing my hips and twirling his waist,
biting down on my lips, I fell to my face.
He turned my head around and said... "I want to bring you
pleasure too."
Suddenly he slowed down and said,
"Is this what you want me to do?"

I answered, "Yes!"
He sped up, about to explode.
He gripped my hips tighter and let it all go.
I didn't want him to stop.
I wanted so much more, still dripping, and all
it was my turn to explore.
"Lay down, baby. It's my turn to play."
He turned and looked at me as now I started to say...
"Don't worry, baby,
I'm gonna take care of you.
You're getting ready to feel amazing soon, so I'm asking you,
"Is this what you want me to do?"

July 15, 1995

TIME WON'T WAIT

Time stand still
so that I can get a second chance.
Time stand still
so that I can meet the perfect man for me.
Every time I turn around,
you're right behind me.
I need a little more time to do things differently.
Don't go too fast 'cause
I'm running out of energy.
Time stand still. Please stand still for me.

I need time to see
all the things I haven't seen...
time slow down, slow down for me.
Time hear me crying, make my life work for me.
I need time to learn to love myself, time to forgive myself.
Everything is so messed up,
time slow down
so I can fix what I broke.
I need time to see all the things I haven't seen. time slow down,
slow down for me.
I need time to be who I was meant to be. Time stand still, please
stand still for me.

I just need more time!

August 14, 2003

"I Got Something To Say"

Why is my love only good when it eases your frustrations but any other time ignored because you don't seem to have the patience? Why can't we make love in all of those little moments we have that are free? I know my yang is good...Oh, you don't like sweet stuff, and my sweet stuff runs too deep? What! You scared? Or is it now you've had just a little too much to drink? Why can't we be kind to one another when no one is around? A kiss on the cheek, say nice things, and throw in a little smile? Fuck that shit you talking 'bout!! Saying it's work, just business, and that's why. That's bullshit! It's not about the business, the problem is you and I. You think that I'm naïve, blind to a lot of things. Well, think again, brotha' because this chic you are about to lose is much smarter than you seem to think. It's sad that you will let pride, stubbornness, and stupidity allow you to lose the best thing you will ever have. Try learning from these experiences and let your actions show the knowledge gained, see if you are given a better path, one much brighter away from all the rain. You must be one of those that think a woman is forever naïve and under the hand of a man, she will always be weak. She holds it down when you can't, making sure everything is all right, she makes sure the foundation is set and that everything is in place and tight. You think I am supposed to?

You forgot one thing, love...I don't owe you! Anyway, you sound stupid, and take them shades off!! We argue because you need to feel like the man but stop being so silly. Sometimes real men need a helping hand. When you look at me, what do you see?

Are there no more attractions here between you and me? You don't have to play it off, don't worry, it's okay because whatever lies in this path I walk, I will walk over it every day. You don't have to talk to me, and you know what...I think you should pack instead. I gotta get up early, so I need to get to bed. This thing between us just isn't going to work, so be sure to get all of your shit, that blue, black, and the yellow shirt. You don't have to worry about finding the key; the locks will be changed right after you leave. Don't worry about a call when you come to grips and start to see. I will not be around to be the next one you deceive...oh, no, no, no, not me! I am strong and smart and will be just fine without you, so no need to try and touch me. It seems as if you want to make me what?? Boo hoo....no time for that. Your ride is waiting, so you need to move fast. Don't try to turn this around on me because you don't see my cry. You drained all of that out of me each time with each lie. By the way, thank you for that. Now my shirts will stay nice and dry. You're gone now...o.k. sweetheart...Goooood Byyyyyyyyye!!!

Bastard!!

December 10, 2013

LIFE BEFORE YOU

Every day seemed like a challenge,
I never thought that I could manage.
My whole world was falling apart all around me,
I never thought another day I would see.
I needed a friend, someone who understood me,
and then you came along
when everyone else was too busy.

Before I met you, I never knew the things that I could do.
Until I met you, I never dared to dream; my dreams were few. So
glad I met you
because now my life is filled with so much joy.

Now I'm living, loving, caring, sharing and this happiness is all
because of you.

Ever since you came into my life,
I know everything is going to be alright.
All of my friends say
they see a brand-new me.
If only they knew, with you,
all of the things that they could be.
I want to tell the world how I feel, so happy and so free.
If they could just see how much

my new friend has done so much for me.

Before I met you, I never knew the things that I could do. Until I
met you, I never dared to dream, my dreams were few.
So glad I met you because now my life is filled with so much joy.

Now I'm living, loving, caring, sharing and this happiness is all
because of you.

December 19, 2001

HOW IT'S GOTTA BE

The love came sooner than later
as time went on, nothing too heavy, nothing too strong...
That's how it's gotta be.

I'm not supposed to love him,
but I can like him a whole, whole lot.
His kind words and soft voice
always seem to hit that right spot!
How can I not fall victim to his game,
his touch, his kiss,
when I'm falling for the way he looks at me,
his dark lips, and that special way that we just click?

The way we talk for hours at a time,
the way that I miss him when he's gone,
but never really wishing he was mine. It's funny...
That's how it's gotta be.

The things we do and say, how quiet and discrete.
Those moments of passion that we share
when no one else is around...
That's how it's gotta be.

To me, he is wonderful,
and this thing of ours is so good.

I don't know how he feels,
I have to just wait and see,
for right now
I have to sit tight because...
This is how it's gotta be.

In him, I've found a special someone,
and I'm not too blind to see
that me loving him and him loving me, that could never be.
If all we could ever be were friends,
then that would be alright with me.
Because for the moment, right here, right now...
This Is Just How It's Gotta Be.

December 19, 2001

LULLABY

Mommy's here, baby. Don't worry,

don't cry.
Come to mama,
and I'll dry your precious eyes.
Lay in my arms
and fall deeply asleep
as I whisper a sweet lullaby
that will cradle you in peace.
Open your eyes!
Oh, but now I'm gone
you can be sure that I'll be back at the crack of dawn.
Nighty-night my love.

September 5, 1994

HEAVENLY LOVE

You were a vision of true love
sent from the heavens that I prayed to every night.
From the first moment, I laid eyes on you;
I instantly knew I wanted you that night.

We talked some and got to know each other very well;
as time passed, our love grew strong,
as if we were under a love spell.

You confessed your love to me
many days and many nights.
I never thought anything to be wrong,
for we would never argue or fight.
Little did I know you were leaving me that night.

I would see you on the days
that we agreed were right for us,
but on the other days, I missed your love
I missed your touch and your kiss so much.

In the days of my despair,
you were nowhere to be found.
I often wondered if someone else was loving you,
was there another love somewhere around?

I think back to the day that we ran into each other
while we were both just casually hanging out.
My thoughts of you having another love
were no longer an insecurity, no longer my doubt.

As the day turned to night
and the night grew old and cold,
I kneeled at the foot of my bed
and cried out prayers to my lord.
I asked him for his guidance and for him to show me the way...

He answered with a soft voice,
and kneeled beside me as he started to say,
"My child, I am here for you. I will help you through this, you see,
but what you will have to do is let him be who he is and put all of
your trust in me."

April 1, 1996

HAPPY ANNIVERSARY

One month ago today

was the day that we met.
A month later, look at us;
who would have ever guessed
that our hands would meet,
and our lips would touch;
I never thought that as the days went by,
I would grow to love you so much.
Looking back now,
I never thought we'd be so close.
I'm glad we met,
glad that there are things about each other we are getting to know.
I guess what I'm trying to say
is that I want to be by your side.
I know it's easier said than done, I can show you, just give me a try.
An anniversary symbolizes togetherness
and holds memories that won't fade.
I want to say to you,
Happy Anniversary
for that moment,
we met one month ago today.

August 19, 1995

A Day Too Late

Today I'm going to be better than I was yesterday.
Today I'm going to change my life because I was told, "it's never
too late."
I'm going to use this time of transformation
for activating, evolving, and progression.
Preparing my mind to excavate my vessel.
Make space for what I learn from the new lessons.
There is just so much that I must do
throughout these days during this time.
I know that during this journey
I will see what I have set out to find.
I can almost hear the winds telling me
to get moving, that I have no choice.
Although I'm not quite ready to go,
it's just that I do not doubt this voice.
Those days will sometimes seem to go
so fast but are not that far away.
Is that enough time? The wind has spoken again,
"It's not too late. Get up, get headed to the finish line."

Live to find you're purpose for living, and never stop looking.
You don't have to be a day too late.

November 14, 2017

The Way I Feel About You

To meet up with you again

was always what I wanted.
To stop my feelings from happening
too late, they have already started.
The way you held me
and your soft touch to my skin, with a touch like that, it's hard not
to sin.
You kissed my lips as if it were your last time; we
savored the moment
I became yours, and you became mine.
Now I think is the time for us to take a stand,
If you walk by my side, I promise to hold your hand.
Times will get hard, and I promise you they will get harder. Over
trial and triumph, together, we will become smarter.
I want you to understand all the things that I will do
to help you see how much I care about you.
It will take more than just words to really make you see
that I was meant for you, and you were meant for me.
Whenever there's something said, something taught,
something read, or something to be fought for...
This is when you will know because I'll be right there. My
friendship is true, and really all I want you to know
is how much I truly care about you...

December 12, 1994

Confused

You look at me and think,

"Why does she like me?"
But you don't think about all the good; from when I look at you
that I see.
You work so hard, you deserve your space,
understanding, and someone to be by your side.
Don't take that kindness for granted, believe me, it's not that easy
to find.
You don't have to be a superstar
or make a lot of money to be with me,
but you do have to be strong,
kind, honest, and hardworking.
All these things are in you, and I see.
I understand that when something good comes your way,
you don't know how to act.
When there's something you're not used to,
you seem to turn your back.
Don't let a good thing pass you by,
I know it's sometimes hard to do.
Sometimes we get so confused,
Are you for me, am I for you?
Don't worry about the things that you can't change,
just let me be a part of your life.
I'm not trying to be the mother of your child,

and I'm not trying to be your wife.
Let's start this off by just being friends,
maybe you'll be a little more comfortable with that.
Hopefully, one day you will see,
I became the best friend you ever had.

June 10, 1995

SURVIVING

---

*Why do people always want to know what I'm doing with my life
or where I'm living?
They say that I don't know what I want to do and that my life is a
waste.
I better figure it out soon.
Well, this is what I say:*

*Have you ever walked in my shoes, been loved, and been hated?
Were you born to my mother, and did you suffer what I suffered
daily?
Were you burned by fire? Did you see the flame? Were you
scorned by your peers?
I tell you what; it hurts just the same.
Just one more mental anguish to overcome ALONE!
Were you violated as a child by those who didn't know you and
those who did?
Did you fight for love and for life even though you were just a kid?
Did you think of suicide, although you were too young to
comprehend the cause and effect?
Did you understand its severity and what it really meant?
Did you have no self-esteem because no one ever told you what it
was?
Did you wander the streets aimlessly, lost and confused through
all the drama and the drugs?*

You see, I am that I am, and I will continue to do what I do...

Searching for a higher power to help get me through each day,
Understanding who I am and that each night I have to pray,
Realizing the realities of a harsh world.
Visualizing a better future
Increasing my chances for success by gaining more knowledge with an open mind
Venerate my elders, respect them, and honor them
Imperfect, understanding that I am
Never giving up on myself or those I love
Guiding those that I can

So, you want to know what I'm doing in my life?

I Am Surviving

May 10, 2000

Tic – Toc

Tic toc, tic toc is all that you hear from the clock on the wall.

Funny how time flies,
leaving no time to finish it all.
Each day that goes by has already become the past.
If daylight could just stay a little longer,
the things we could not finish,
we could finish at last.

Funny how time flies
even when you're not having so much fun.

The clock is still ticking
as we try to get so much done
....no time ....no time...

Time waits for no man,
and this, I think we all know,
so, use your time wisely
because before you know it,
it's' time to go.......
We just need a little more time to finish the things we start.

So that we can stop rushing,
taking some time out to rest our hearts.

Tic...toc... Tick...toc...

Is all that you hear from the clock on the wall?

April 6, 2006

REDEEMED

I never thought in a million years that I would be the one to
fulfill all my dreams, face all my fears and come out number one.
I never thought these things could be true,
for I never believed in me, but with the knowledge that I now have
gained
I can become anything, times three!
I have strengthened my character,
my body and my mind.
I have found a brand new me.
I have a heavenly friend who is with me on the front line
...fighting my battles, and he is always on time.
My smile is new.
My mind is renewed, and my soul has found a new home.
In this place that I call love, I am no longer alone.
I am glad that my eyes are no longer blinded,
that my vision is perfect and clear.
So many of you want this love
but are afraid to come near.
Let him love you; it doesn't hurt a bit.
Just open your arms and let him come in.
What I've found, I'm never letting go...
He'll always love me, and this I know.

July 4, 2002

WHY DO I CRY?

I cry because I'm sad inside,

making hasty decisions and having to decide;

I cry...

because I saw your pain when I packed my bags and ran away, I

cry...

because I saw your head in your hands,

trying to understand "why"

when you knew you were being a good man,

I cry...

you didn't deserve what I did to your heart,

and maybe my hasty decisions were not all that smart.

I'm crying...

I live in a world of pain and trouble,

a world of anger and lies.

Ask me "why I hurt inside,"

the answer to your question,

"That is why I cry."

You've brought nothing but happiness, serenity, and sanity into

my life;

I've grown from this experience and learned

"I need to fight."

Because I know that the end for us is near,

leaving nothing else in me but heartache and fear.

I cry...

no one has ever looked at me
the way that you have, put my heart at ease
and lent a helping hand so,
I cry...
please know that all I have said and done was sincere and from
the heart.
I'm going to seek a brand-new life and make a brand-new start.
Writing this, I feel queasy inside,
and teary-eyed as well,
I wanted so badly to make you happy,
and I hope that you could tell.
These are my last words to you from my heart and soul deep down
inside;
I've grown to have a strong love for you and as I walk away I still
cry.

June 24, 2000

AMONI

Another day is gone.
Another hour has passed by
each day I sit and think of you
another tear, I cry.

My heart is full of pain and
sadness,
but happiness is there too.
Some of the joys our lives used to have,
we lost it all when we lost you.

You're gone to a place where there is no hate
and color has no name.
A place where there is no sorrow,
nothing but love, no heartache, no pain.

You're gone to that special place,
where nothing there goes wrong.
In the arms of an entity who will take care of you
and help you to help us be strong.

I want you to know that I love you, no matter
how far apart we are.

You were my only little brother AMONI.

And you will always hold a special place in my heart.

Your sisters will always love you.

Date: the day after his passing in 1995
In memory of Amoni Ja'quan Porter, age11 I am so happy I had
the opportunity to meet my
brother. A strong bond and a beautiful friendship built in such
a short period of time. It was a pleasure Amoni and you are
truly missed, I love you!

BONDED

My mountain has fallen...way too far down.
Time to start over
and build it back up from the ground.
I will not stop or give up in any downfall or hard time, this is no
exception so no, not this time.
I sit back and just watch while I view the clock and tilt my bottle of
wine.
Same words over and over again you speak,
mostly your little white lies and constant deceit.
All because you think I don't know,
can't hear and can't see,
but trust when I tell you I see all of the inconsistencies.
Now I guess you sit and assume
I have nothing to argue against your so-called validity.
As much as you want me to believe you,
I dare myself to even conceive to.
What you will feel and see one day is that,
it is not what you do but how you do.
A woman stuck in that trained,
embedded vision of whom she is supposed to be, not me...
Instant rejection to the old seat; a new one has been taken over by
me.
Constant inner conflictions
and battles trying to tear the inner me....
I have to stay focused, on point, and ready.

A fight that turned into a war is now surfaced,
up and ready to break down the door,
but I will stay grounded; keep my feet on the floor.
Let no one else in; they can find the path that is their own,
with or without a BOND,
there is no guarantee that path will keep them coming home.
I'm not property. Leave be my belongings and or other things
If destruction is what you have in mind.
Since I'm all me, myself, and I,
I'll work it in thy own way, in thy own time.
Headaches and heartaches are not worth the mental,
emotional, financial, infidelity, lies & distress
that come while holding down the line.
What progression has really been made?
What has truly been gained in all of this time?
Is this not truly a sign?
Is this not truly a test to our time?
You come to me with one issue that is important,
but absolutely nothing towards all that has been.
Communication, in the little frustrating way that you say it,
could break us, but doesn't even hold up to all of your past and
present bullshit.
The same shit you portray and relay throughout this entire round
doesn't make sense. When I portray some of it, when coming from
me,
it's suddenly not as sound and senseless.
That's okay - I'm up and again already moving forward.
I say I've done my part and continue onward.
Blacked out this here what seems to be your excuse for all of what's
wrong.

*This is now becoming one more experience that has helped in
making me strong.
I'm getting it back together, headed straight to the finish line.
Didn't see you by my side, so....okay......oh well....
I must leave you in the dust that had to be left behind.
Once again to you, I must say there is no more crying.
No need for the "Why" because the only thing I will say to you now
is..... Bye Bye.....*

August 16, 2017